THE JOURNEY OF ENGLISH

BY DONNA BROOK

ILLUSTRATED BY JEAN DAY ZALLINGER

CLARION BOOKS ✤ *NEW YORK*

The author thanks faculty and students from Saint Ann's School in Brooklyn, New York, especially Paul O'Rourke, Nuar Alsadir, Gail Brousal, Robert Henneman, Jack McShane, and Diana Raimondi. Thank you also to Linda Overton and Nancy Stauffer for professional advice.

For my parents
—D.B.

For R.F.Z.
For Dorothy and Anne
—J.D.Z.

Clarion Books
a Houghton Mifflin Company imprint
215 Park Avenue South, New York, NY 10003
Text copyright © 1998 by Donna Brook
Illustrations copyright © 1998 by Jean Day Zallinger

The illustrations for this book were executed in watercolor and color pencils.
The text is set in 13.5/18-point Horley oldstyle.

Printed in the USA.

Library of Congress Cataloging-in-Publication Data

Brook, Donna.
The journey of English / by Donna Brook ; illustrated by Jean Day Zallinger.
p.   cm.
Includes bibliographical references.
ISBN 0-395-71211-4
1. English language—History—Juvenile literature. I. Zallinger, Jean. II. Title.
PE1072.B727   1998
420'.9—DC20   95-52354
CIP
AC

WOZ   10 9 8 7 6 5 4 3 2 1

English is by far the most popular language of the thousands spoken in the world today. Found all over the globe, English is a world language of business, government, and education. Used on six continents, English is an official or important language in over eighty countries. Over three-fourths of the world's mail is in English. More than two-thirds of the world's scientists write articles and books about their findings in English.

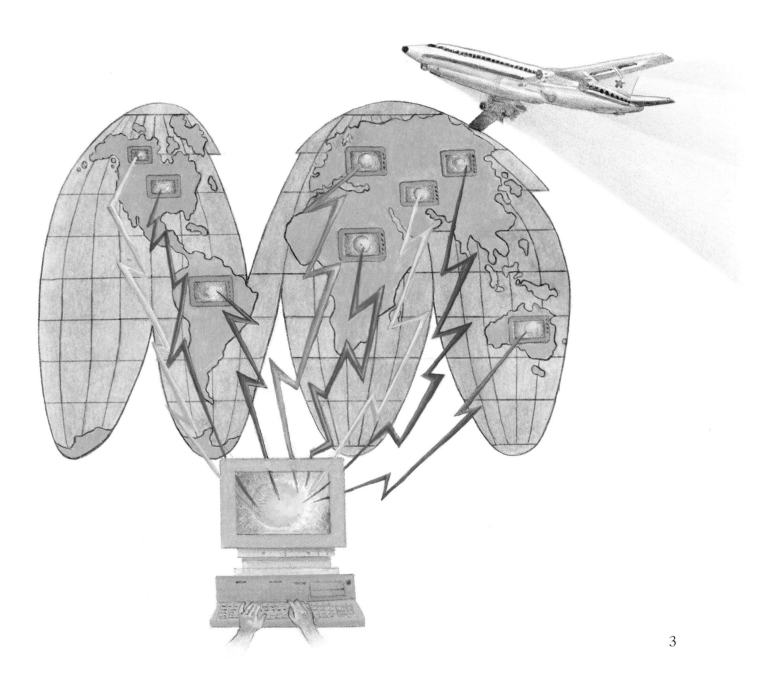

About 400 million people speak English as their first language, or mother tongue. It is the second or official language for more than 500 million others. Another few hundred million people are fluent in English as a foreign language. Add all these people up and English has well over a billion speakers. In quite a few countries, such as India, which has 768 million people, English is the official language in which all of the country's business is conducted. But only 70 million people can actually speak English to some degree or other. So, as in almost all of the world, in India gaining education, power, and wealth means learning English.

In addition to being used in so many countries, today's English has more words than any other language. There are over a billion English words. Actually, only about 200,000 of these words are used regularly, but that is twice the number of French words commonly used. This huge choice of English words makes it easier for a person to say or write exactly what she or he means.

With all the people and words that English has today, it is hard to imagine its beginnings. Going back to prehistoric times, many languages, including English, started near the present border between Europe and Asia.

NORTH SEA

BALTIC SEA

BLACK SE

MEDITERRANEAN SEA

About 3000 B.C., tribes that lived in the area of today's Siberia spoke one language, now called Indo-European. These tribes kept moving farther away from one another. As the groups wandered over bigger areas and became more isolated from each other, each tribe's language changed in a different way. This created many separate languages. Modern languages that may seem nothing at all like one another still belong to the Indo-European language family because of this common source.

INDO-EUROPEAN

CASPIAN SEA

A ALPHA (AH)
B BETA (B)
Γ GAMMA (G)
GREEK

A (AH)
B (CH)
SANSKRIT

A A (AE)
Б B
Д D
CYRILLIC

By 2000 B.C., the Indo-European groups had become so removed from one another that their common origin had been completely forgotten, and the Indo-European language itself completely disappeared. The prehistoric existence of Indo-European was rediscovered only in the last few hundred years, but traces of this one origin can be found in Celtic, Anglo-Saxon, French, Latin, and Greek. All these languages in their turn became important ancestors of today's English, whose specific development began roughly sixteen hundred years ago.

By A.D. 400, a group called the Celts had been living on a small uncivilized island off the coast of Europe, the place we now call England, for at least a thousand years. For about the last four hundred of these years, the vast Roman Empire had ruled the Celts, calling the area Britannia because the natives called themselves Britons. The Romans had brought excellent roads, good administration, and many new things that made the Celts' very simple lives better. (We see this from a few of the words the Celts borrowed from the Romans' language, Latin, for things that were new to them: *table, pillow,* and *wine.*) The Roman occupation was the first of three introductions of Latin into England, but the one with the least impact on English.

Lead Pipes

Pewter

Tin Mask

Great Bath   A.D. 122–126

In A.D. 395, Rome faced increasing problems at home and its empire began to crumble, so the Roman soldiers and officials withdrew and left the Celts to their fate. Tribes such as the Angles and Saxons, who lived in what is now northern Europe, especially Germany, took advantage of the Roman departure and began to invade the inviting fields of England almost immediately.

Hadrian's Wall
Built in A.D. 122–126

After the Angles (who gave their name to England) and the Saxons conquered England, their language, called Anglo-Saxon, began to replace Celtic. Eventually, only traces of the Celtic language remained in England, mainly as place names—like the rivers *Thames* and *Avon,* the cities *London* and *York*—and personal names like *Alan, Donald,* and *Eileen.* (*Ronald McDonald* is a 100 percent Celtic name.) However, many Celts had fled the invaders to what is now Wales, Ireland, Scotland, and Brittany in France, and the Celtic language survived in those places, becoming many related tongues. Today Welsh is spoken by about half a million people, 20 percent of the population in Wales. Irish Gaelic has about 100,000 speakers in Ireland. Scottish Gaelic has some 80,000 speakers in Scotland, and Breton is spoken on France's north-west coast by an estimated half a million people.

13

ROMAN BRITAIN

CALEDONES

VENICONES

ANTONINE WALL

DAMNONII

VOTADINI

SELGOVE

NOVANTAE

HADRIAN'S WALL

BRIGANTES

PARISI

ORDOVICES

CORITANI

CORNOVII

ICENI

CATUVELLAUNI

LONDINIUM
TRADING CENTER

FRONTIER
UNDER
CLAUDIUS

The Germanic tribes had become established in England by the end of the sixth century, marrying, enslaving, or driving out the Celts. Then Viking invaders from Denmark, also known as Norsemen, began to arrive, beginning in 787 A.D. Between 850 and 1050 A.D., the Vikings mixed with the Anglo-Saxons, marrying Anglo-Saxon-speaking women and teaching their wives their Scandinavian language, called Norse.

TIW
(Tuesday)

The resulting mix of Anglo-Saxon and Norse is called Old English, which is very different from today's English in pronunciation, vocabulary, word order, and many other features. However, Old English gives us a lot of our common words, such as *at*, *brother*, *but*, *eat*, *man*, and *sleep*. It also gives us names for six days of the week. *Tuesday* comes from the Saxon god of war, Tiw. The chief god, Woden, and his wife, Frigga, give us *Wednesday* and *Friday*. Anglo-Saxon words for sun and moon give us *Sunday* and *Monday*. *Thursday* is from the god of thunder, known as Thunor or Thor in Norse. *Saturday* is from the Roman god Saturn.

16

FRIGGA
(Friday)

WODEN
(Wednesday)

17

THOR
(Thursday)

SATURN
(Saturday)

As you can see from these names for the days of the week, the Anglo-Saxons believed in many gods. The Pope sent the monk Augustine to England in A.D. 597 to establish monasteries and to convert people to Christianity. This second introduction of Latin (the first was when the Romans ruled Britannia) gives us words such as *altar, angel, ark, candle, hymn, minister, noon, nun, purple, rule, school, silk,* and *temple.*

HELIOS the Sun God
(Sunday)

SELENE the Moon Goddess
(Monday)

St. Augustine meets the Juke King of Canterbury

19

In 1066, Normans from France won the Battle of Hastings, conquering the Anglo-Saxons. French then became the language of England's rulers. Old English remained the language of the people they ruled, who were farmers and servants. For three hundred years, the majority of the population spoke Old English while learning some French, and the powerful minority of rulers spoke French, learning enough Old English to give orders to their subjects. This is why so many of our words for government come from French. *Authority, council, crown, empire, judge, jury, liberty, mayor, parliament, prince, tax, treaty,* and *treasurer* are just a few of them.

NORMAN CONQUESTS, 1066–1087

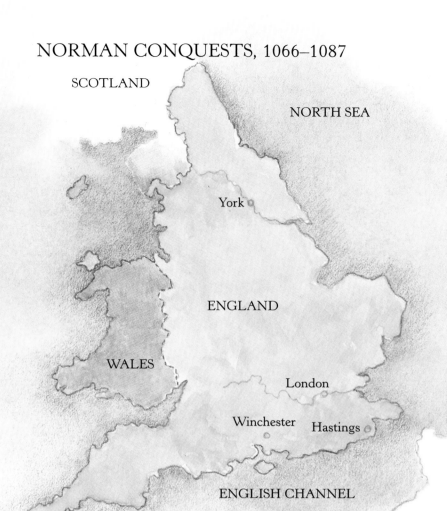

SCOTLAND

NORTH SEA

York

ENGLAND

WALES

London

Winchester   Hastings

ENGLISH CHANNEL

hIC EXEVNT:CABALII   DENAVIBVS ⁓ EThIC:MILITES: FESTINA Q VERV NT:hE

Of course, as time passed, Normans and Anglo-Saxons mixed socially and married each other, just as Vikings and Anglo-Saxons had. The plague, a deadly disease carried by fleas on rats, killed over a third of the population in a few years, mainly from 1347 to 1351, and caused the social order to break down. Surviving Anglo-Saxons began to rise into the ruling class, carrying their language with them. By 1362, Middle English, a mix of French and Old English, was the standard language of England.

ΑΒΓΔΕΖΗΘΙΚΛΜ
ΝΞΟΠΡΣΤΥΦΧΨΩ  GREEK

ABCDEFGHI·KLM
NOPQRST·V·XYZ  ROMAN

ABCDEFGHIJKLM
NOPQRSTUVWXYZ  MODERN ENGLISH

From roughly 1300 to 1600, during a period called the Renaissance, the vast knowledge of ancient Rome and Greece was recovered. Ten thousand to twelve thousand new English words were invented in the sixteenth century alone. Many of these words were shaped from Latin and Greek because of the prestige these languages had. Others were just made up by combining existing words.

Today, between 60 and 70 percent, or perhaps even more, of English words come from Latin, and about 15 percent come from Greek. The words that come from Old English, then, make up only a small percentage of the whole vocabulary of English. But, since these plain Anglo-Saxon words are the base of everyday conversation, they are the words most frequently used in our speech. So it is easy to miss the contributions of ancient Greece and Rome.

Long before the English language began, the Greeks (whose greatest period was around the fifth century before Christ) and the Romans had each had a very impressive civilization and a powerful empire. The Greeks passed on much learning to the Romans. Roman citizens knew not only their own language, Latin, but Greek too, for their teachers were Greek slaves. After the Roman Empire fell, much knowledge was "lost," forgotten by most people but kept alive mainly by Christian monks who lived in isolated monasteries.

HIPPOCRATES
Medicine

ARCHIMEDES
Mathematics

EUCLID
Geometry

Every monastery in England and Europe had a library and a scriptorium, where trained monks carefully copied important ancient Greek and Latin books by hand. Also, since every university in Europe used Latin as the language of instruction during the Middle Ages (the period between the fall of Rome and the rise of the Renaissance), Latin was the language of both religious and earthly knowledge. It was waiting to be rediscovered when the Middle or Dark Ages, a time of war and disorganization in Europe, finally passed.

SIR THOMAS MORE
1478–1535

GEOFFREY CHAUCER
1342–1400

FRANCIS BACON
1561–1626

EDMUND SPENSER
1552–1599

The third and most important introduction of Latin into English was in the Renaissance. During this period, a unique feature of today's English, with its huge vocabulary, became established. One basic meaning could be expressed by three different English words that came from three sources—Anglo-Saxon, French, and Latin. Here are a few examples:

ANGLO-SAXON	FRENCH	LATIN
fear	terror	trepidation
win	succeed	triumph
kingly	royal	regal
holy	sacred	consecrated

26

ANDREAS VESALIUS
1514–1564

LEONARDO DA VINCI
1452–1519

SIR FRANCIS DRAKE
1540–1596

GALILEO GALILEI
1564–1642

Also, during the Renaissance, Greek and Latin became increasingly important influences on English because the ancient civilizations of Greece and Rome had contributed so much to scientific knowledge. Many scientific words come from Greek and Latin, including *atmosphere, pneumonia, skeleton, species, thermometer,* and *virus.*

The sciences of medicine and biology still use Latin today to classify diseases, animals, plants, and so on without confusion. For example, one small animal is known by several names throughout America, but whether it is a "woodchuck" or a "groundhog" or a "marmot" to other people, it is always *Marmota monax* to scientists.

The Renaissance was an exciting period of invention, discovery, literature, and travel. Columbus and other explorers sailed to discover the New World, bringing back new foods and new words, like *potato*. In 1476, William Caxton introduced the printing press into England. Books became less expensive and more plentiful, so more and more people learned to read English. (It was an English without spelling rules or punctuation, but it was now an English understandable today.)

William Shakespeare (1564–1616) wrote plays and poems that contributed many words to English. He had a vocabulary of over thirty thousand words by the time he was done writing. A few examples from Shakespeare are *assassination, bump, lonely, in the mind's eye,* and *not budge an inch.*

All experts on the history of English agree that the big influences on the language near the end of the Renaissance were Shakespeare and the King James Bible of 1611, which gave us many expressions such as *the apple of his eye, the salt of the earth,* and *eat sour grapes.* Another important source was *The Book of Common Prayer,* first compiled in 1549.

JOHANNES GUTENBERG
1400–1468?
First European to Print
with Movable Type

WILLIAM CAXTON
1422–1491
First English Printer

15th Century Printing Press

One last major event separates the English we speak today, Modern English, from Middle English. This event is called The Great Vowel Shift, and it took place around 1400 to 1450. The Great Vowel Shift meant that many words got new pronunciations because their vowel sounds changed in just a few generations. For instance, in Middle English, *go* rhymed with *law*. Today, *go* rhymes with *low*. Once *good* rhymed with *rode*, not with *hood*. The Shift affected nearly all the long vowel sounds in this way. Nobody knows why it happened.

MIDDLE
ENGLISH
1150 – 1500

Ther is much feasting in this moneth but few the better for it.

This development of English before 1600 is only half the story. How did English move from its little island to world popularity? The answer is simple. It traveled with the people who spoke it.

As soon as ships could sail far enough, European countries began to claim new territories. Great Britain established colonies in the New World, and in time, English became the official language of the United States of America.

31

Canada has two languages, French and English, because both France and England sent settlers there. America's Southwest has Spanish place names because Spain sent settlers to New Mexico and Texas. Spanish is spoken in most countries of Central and South America because Spain ruled there once.

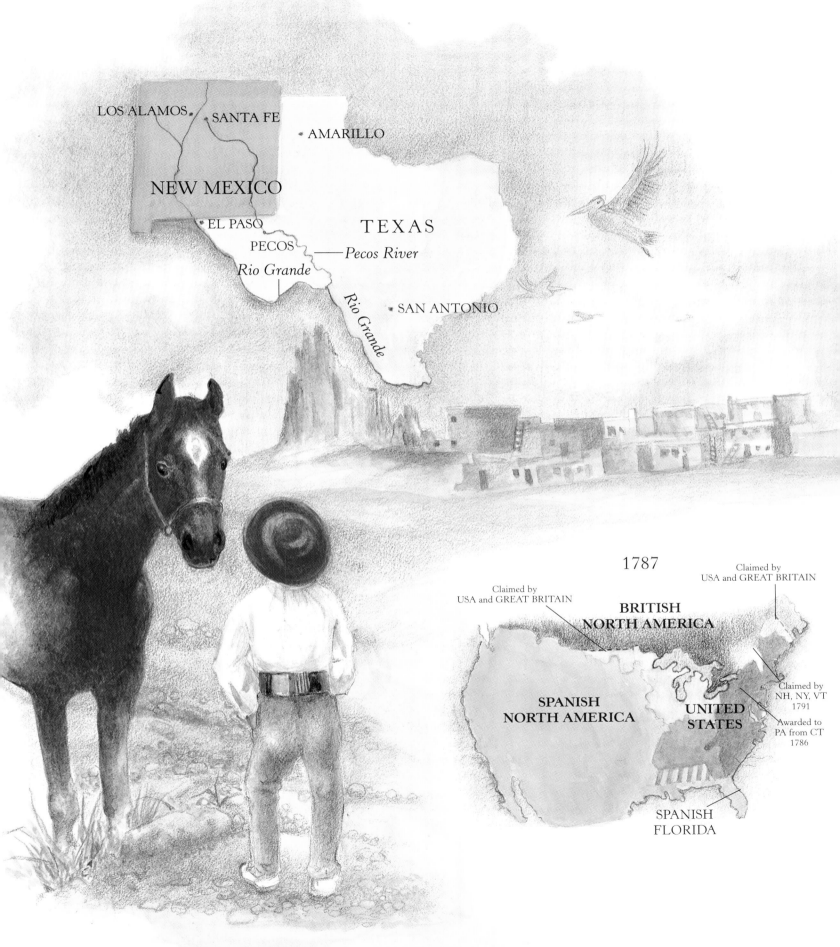

LOS ALAMOS · SANTA FE

· AMARILLO

NEW MEXICO

· EL PASO

TEXAS

PECOS — *Pecos River*

Rio Grande

Rio Grande

· SAN ANTONIO

1787

Claimed by
USA and GREAT BRITAIN

Claimed by
USA and GREAT BRITAIN

BRITISH
NORTH AMERICA

SPANISH
NORTH AMERICA

UNITED
STATES

Claimed by
NH, NY, VT
1791

Awarded to
PA from CT
1786

SPANISH
FLORIDA

When it came to establishing colonies, though, no one topped the English. People used to say, "The sun never sets on the British Empire," because England's empire was on so many continents. England sent settlers to Australia and New Zealand, which are now English-speaking countries. Conquests in Africa, Asia, and the Caribbean led to the establishment of English as an official language in countries all over the world.

NORTHERN
TERRITORY

WESTERN
AUSTRALIA

QUEENSLAND

SOUTH
AUSTRALIA

NEW
SOUTH
WALES

Kiwi

NEW ZEALAND

When the British came to a place, they acquired and used some of the words that the natives were already using. For example, the words *hickory, moose, skunk,* and *tobacco* are North American Indian words. Over half of American states' names are from Native American languages. *Alabama, Alaska, Connecticut, Idaho, Massachusetts, Oklahoma,* and *Tennessee* are just a few of them.

AUSTRALIA

CUBA

HISPANIOLA

PUERTO
RICO

From Australia, we get *kangaroo* and *boomerang.* Words from the Caribbean include *hammock* and *hurricane.* India contributed *cashmere, jungle,* and *sugar.* Africa gave *canary, yam,* and *banana.* Mostly, though, English pushed the native languages aside. It was much easier to govern people in one language, the ruler's language, than in hundreds of local languages.

SUGAR

INDIA

AFRICA

37

As the places that Great Britain had colonized became independent countries, English was kept as a nation's official language for several reasons. Often, a country had so many small language groups of its own that communication among all its citizens was easier in one common language, English. Picking English also solved any problems about jealousy, which might have caused tensions if any one local group's language were singled out. Also, choosing English made it easier for a country to communicate with all the other places that used English.

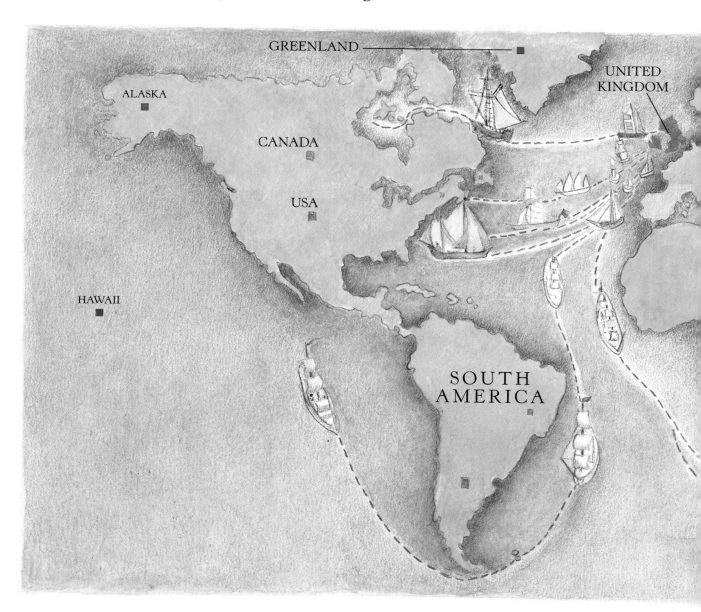

Although British English has spread all over the world, American English has had a big impact in the last fifty years. The United States has become the most powerful country in the world, so its language has become very popular. All over the globe, people say *OK*, a very American expression, whether or not they say another word in English.

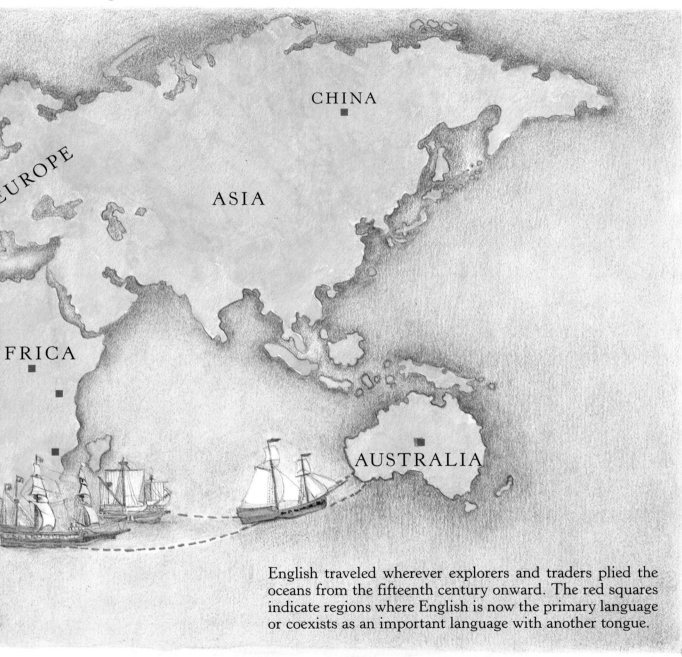

English traveled wherever explorers and traders plied the oceans from the fifteenth century onward. The red squares indicate regions where English is now the primary language or coexists as an important language with another tongue.

Perhaps today we should speak of many kinds of English. Just compare some American words with the words used in Great Britain.

No one knows what the future of English will be. Some experts predict that British English and American English will become so different from each other that at some

lorry

truck

future date Americans and Britons will have a very hard time understanding each other. Different accents and different words may make the English in the USA very unlike that in Great Britain, India, or South Africa. Years in the future, maybe these will become separate languages. Maybe not.

Although English will probably be more and more influenced by new communication devices that can move language without moving people (films, TV, computer networks, etc.), patterns of immigration and birth rates will still be important. It has been estimated that by the year 2056 a minority of American citizens will be of European heritage. The rest will be descendants of African, Asian, Native, and Latin Americans. Spanish will have an increasing influence in America, for people from Mexico, Puerto Rico, and Central and South America are moving north. The African-American influence on American English has already given us many well-known words and phrases.

The Big Apple for New York City is one. Others are *big shot, check it out, cold-blooded, gumbo, jazz,* and *out to lunch.*

English came into existence by absorbing other languages such as Norse and French. It has always borrowed words from other languages—such as *camel* from Hebrew, *piano* from Italian, and *zero* from Arabic. Meanwhile, new meanings keep attaching themselves to old words. Once a mouse was a tiny animal that ate cheese. Now a computer comes with a different kind of *mouse.* All that is certain is that English is always changing and will always keep changing.

SIR JAMES MURRAY
1837–1915

NOAH WEBSTER
1758–1843

DR. SAMUEL JOHNSON
1709–1784

DICTIONARIES

A good up-to-date dictionary is very important. It gives a word's pronunciation, meaning, and history. It tells how a word is divided into syllables, whether or not it is capitalized, and how it is used in a sentence.

English lexicography (the making of dictionaries) began with lists of difficult or foreign words used by people who were traveling or trying to understand some technical or rare term. In 1604, the first English "dictionary of hard words" was compiled, but dictionaries as they are today really began with Samuel Johnson in 1755. Johnson's *Dictionary of the English Language* gave the definitions for over forty thousand words, using quotations from the best authors to illustrate meanings. His was the first attempt to give an organized record of the whole language, and it set up the idea of a dictionary as an authority that anyone could consult.

Noah Webster published the first important description of American English in his *An American Dictionary of the English Language*, 1828, and gave the English spoken in North America a clear identity.

But probably the prize for devotion to a dictionary goes to James Murray (1837–1915). Murray, the first editor of the *Oxford English Dictionary* (the *OED*), planned the whole project and worked on it until his death. The completed work held 424,825 entries when it was published in 1933. It had taken forty-four years to finish and, during that time, sections had appeared in 125 installments. But, as soon as it was all put together, people immediately began to update and revise it to keep pace with the changes happening in English. There were several supplements, and in 1989 a revised *OED* was published. Because the twenty volumes of the *OED* use so much space and cost so much, many libraries have a one-volume version with print so small that it can be read only with a strong magnifying glass.

Some Clues to Word Origin from Spelling

If a word has a *gh* that is silent—think Anglo-Saxon. EXAMPLES: fight, sight, high, sign, bought, thought, ought, caught, taught, naughty

If a one- or two-syllable word begins with a silent letter—think Anglo-Saxon. EXAMPLES: knee, knob, knuckle, knight, gnaw, gnarl, gnat, gnash, wrist, wrinkle, wrench, wrong

If a word begins with *sk* or *sc*—think Norse. EXAMPLES: scatter, scare, scrape, skirt, skin, sky, scalp, scold, skit

If a two-syllable word ends in *ain*—think French. EXAMPLES: mountain, fountain, certain

If a word has *ci* pronounced *sh*—think French. EXAMPLES: gracious, delicious, precious

If a word begins with a silent *p*—think Greek. EXAMPLES: psychology, psychiatric, pneumonia

If a word has *ph* pronounced as *f*—think Greek. EXAMPLES: philosophy, philanderer

Some Clues to Word Origin from Meaning

If a word is about a basic of life—think Anglo-Saxon. EXAMPLES: fire, foot, hate, help, love, meat, wife

If a word is a conjunction, pronoun, or preposition—think Anglo-Saxon. EXAMPLES: and, but, for, from, he, him, his, in

If a word is about government or law—think French. EXAMPLES: attorney, crime, court, government, nation, property, royal, state

If a word is about cooking or food—think French. EXAMPLES: beef, boil, broil, fry, gravy, pork, roast, salad, taste

If a word is about the church—think Latin. EXAMPLES: cross, martyr, mass, monk, paradise, pope, priest

If a word is the name of a month or planet—think Latin. EXAMPLES: all twelve months and all but one planet (Uranus is from Greek)

If a word is about a subject in school—think Greek. EXAMPLES: arithmetic, astronomy, biology, geography, history

Bibliography

Books of Particular Interest to Young Readers and Their Teachers

Beal, George. *The Kingfisher Book of Words.* New York: Grisewood & Dempsey, 1992.

Cooper, Kay. *Why Do You Speak As You Do? A Guide to World Languages.* New York: Walker and Company, 1992.

Klausner, Janet. *Talk About English: How Words Travel and Change.* New York: Crowell, 1990.

Morwood, James, and Mark Warman. *Our Greek and Latin Roots.* Cambridge, England: Cambridge University Press (*Awareness of Language* series, ed. Eric Hawkins), 1990.

Papp, Joseph, and Elizabeth Kirkland. *Shakespeare Alive!* New York: Bantam, 1988.

Robinson, Sandra R. *Origins: Volume 1, Bringing Words to Life* and *Origins: Volume 2, The Word Families.* New York: Teachers & Writers Collaborative, 1989.

Books of General Interest

Bryson, Bill. *The Mother Tongue: English & How It Got That Way.* New York: Morrow, 1990.

———. *Made in America: An Informal History of the English Language in the United States.* New York: Morrow, 1994.

Burchfield, Robert. *The English Language.* New York: Oxford, 1987.

———. *Unlocking the English Language.* New York: Hill & Wang, 1991.

Claiborne, Robert. *Our Marvelous Native Tongue.* New York: Times Books, 1983.

———. *The Roots of English.* New York: Times Books, 1989.

Crystal, David. *The Cambridge Encyclopedia of Language,* 1987. Revised 1995. New York: Cambridge University Press.

Fromkin, Victoria, and Robert Rodman. *An Introduction to Language,* Third Edition. New York: Holt, Rinehart, and Winston, 1983.

Funk, Charles Earle. *2107 Curious Word Origins, Sayings & Expressions from White Elephants to Song Dance.* New York: Galahad Books, 1993.

Major, Clarence. *Juba to Jive: A Dictionary of African-American Slang.* New York: Penguin, 1994.

Maleska, Eugene T. *A Pleasure in Words.* New York: Simon & Schuster, 1981.

McArthur, Tom, ed. *The Oxford Companion to the English Language.* New York: Oxford University Press, 1992.

McCrum, Robert, William Cran, and Robert McNeil. *The Story of English.* New York: Penguin, 1987.

Pickering, David, *et al. Brewer's Dictionary of Twentieth-Century Phrase and Fable.* Boston: Houghton Mifflin, 1992.

Thorne, Tony. *The Dictionary of Contemporary Slang.* New York: Pantheon, 1990.

INDEX